A POETIC JOURNEY

Into the

UNSPOKEN

STORIES OF THE

MIND, BODY & SOUL.

BY

LLOYD "BLACK-STONE" LEITCH.

INTRODUCTION

The Unspoken Stories of the MIND, BODY & SOUL is a creative masterpiece that captures; as well as embodies the Rhythms and the emotional flows of life, love, and liberative imagination. These figurative experiences allow you to embark on a surreal adventure. Be prepared to be consumed by reflective topics, stimulating ideas, and mentally tap into unforgettable moments.

TABLES OF CONTENTS

STEPPING OUT OF MY COMFORT ZONE

Removing my shackles, restraints and hindrances.

I stepped out of my comfort zone.

The shoelaces of obstacles started screaming when I left them loose.

Feeling nervous and scared at times because the road seemed challenging.

Trusting that the universe has a master plan when all I needed to do was stand up and start being the person I needed to.

Stepping out of the comfort zone does not require great expertise and skill, it only requires your effort and appreciates your will.

Trusting the process may seem difficult at times, as you step into the unknown the broken bottles and stones...cut away at your feet like slicing pineapples.

Deep down inside there's a burning desire to win ,as you draw for your strength and the motivation from within. Never losing your focus the mission is in plain sight; while watching the steps as you navigate just right.

I stepped out of my comfort zone not to be perfect than anyone else, but because I understood risk; and challenge was the only thing yielding a treasure chest.

So, as I implore you to take the first steps and give it a try, just remember stepping out of your comfort zone takes you on a magnitude that is beyond your heights.

Just step out of your zone! and leave the rest alone.

TAKEN FOR GRANTED

Were you ever taken for granted and if yes how did it make you feel? did it make you feel unseen, unheard and invisible to the world you valued possessing an unlikely appeal?

Were there times you were looked down upon, or never ,taken seriously at times, and even brushed aside like garbage taken by the wind and its rides.?

Were you ever taken for granted? by the people you cherish, love and look up to. Maybe some friends, families and spouses you saw their crystals through and through.

At times you may sit alone in the dark wondering will it ever get better, maybe you'll sit and write in your journal, diary or even seek help in the matter.

Never be around the people who will take you for granted, especially those refusing to see your worth and value. Instead, be of good Courage whilst standing your ground tapping into your inner virtue.

Most of all never take your life for granted, because you are here for a reason. You would have to figure out yourself, your gift and purpose so that you can blossom into your season.

So, hurry up! The clock is ticking and the journey is short; take nothing for granted but with wisdom, knowledge and understanding use these tools to never get stranded.

Imagine being sown like a seed in the ground growing big, mighty, strong and solid. Like the oaks that live in the woods by Mother nature's choice they are planted.

YOU ARE MORE THAN ENOUGH

The days you reflect on how far you've come feeling like a loser and the prizes you have not won. You go all in, hoping deeply to be seen. But the more that you're trying you are always treated as if you were mean.

You suck it up at times and try to be a bigger and better person. Disregarded, abused and disrespected some situations just seemed to worsen.

You question if you're really enough, are the thoughts which often plague the mind. But refused to give up even when failing countless times.

I'm here to tell you..you are more than enough! you were born exceptional, and you were built tough. The things that come at you will never have a hold, because deep down inside you are precious and worth more than gold.

I hope this part of the poem lifts you up and strengthens your spirit, because what's about to happen is predestined for you to win it. So raise up your chin and lift up your head. The brightness is about to begin, "You are more than enough!" Yes, and that's what I said.

Never rely on what others think of you because they don't know who they are, and their aim is to distract you. So, find peace, strength and humility from within, I know that you are loved because you have no replacement or a twin.

Indeed, "YOU" are more than enough!

HEADSPACE

Why rent space in our heads for the unruly tenants of stress; worry fatigue and frustrations only create a bigger mess.

Unwanted furniture looks like doubt, fear and uncertainty; while curtains draped at the windows continuously shape deeper...timidities.

Rented space of negatives was given an eviction without notice, no unnecessary drama to start up just positives, clarity and purpose.

Never allowing trespassers around the perimeters of your mind, especially those idle whispers who spew malicious intent and grime.

Invitations for bidding to the things which offer growth, availability reserved for VIP's whose occupancy increases the worth.

Do not abandon the space inside your head for Crackheads, Bums and Hobos. Instead fill the void with meaningful goals, whilst trying new things and learn more.

LOVE IS AN ACTION

Love is an action!, this, I honestly agree .Whether it's in the form of emotion, character or charity. Not a fairytale story most imagine or believe.

Love is reflective because it shows and teaches a lot about who we are. Whilst on the other hand we demand and expect others to give it freely. Whether they are near or afar.

Love is not lust which is a fleeting pleasure, it constantly looks and waits up for safety at night; like a mother welcoming a son or a daughter.

Love is not violence or brings death, misery and suffering, its truth is kindness amongst many of its spiritual offerings.

Love is not selfishness which a lot seem to misconstrue, instead love is selflessness in acts of thankfulness, gratitude and compassion in showing virtue.

Finally love can come in many forms, shapes or even fashions but its truest value of acceptance and acknowledgement remains still an action.

- *Love is patient and kind love does not envy, or boast is not arrogant or rude.*

- *It does not insist on its own way, it is not irritable or resentful.*

- *Love bears all things, believes all things, hopes all things and endures all things.*

- *It does not rejoice in wrongdoing but rejoices in truth.*

- *love never ends.*

These words are from first Corinthians chapter 13 verses 4 – 8. So, love positively.

TRUTH SERUM

Action! the Clapper board strikes and the camera starts rolling...

Under the spotlight sitting on the chair, eyes were squinting from the piercing truth and glares.

Nervously, pondering awaiting questions unknown, mind traversing the cosmos seeking messages for the soul.

First question!

Do you love yourself and are you proud of who you are, or are you ashamed of keeping yourself distant and afar?

Truth serum; Flowing up and racing through my veins, thoughts in turmoil trying to remain in frame.

Second question!

Do you like what you see when you look into the mirror?

Truth serum; Reflecting on the reflections of my character and variant personalities. Creating masks and hiding cracks, smearing my imperfections, impressions sold.

Third question!

Do you consider yourself perfect or leave room for imperfections and improvements?

Truth serum; Eyes watering as guilt festers and memory surface. Inner consciousness permeates the realities, wetting the inconsiderable judgements of self, void of individual scrutiny.

Last question!

Are you happy with the person you have become?

Truth serum; Overall analysis of the 'Heart, Mind, Body and Soul' leaves conscious truths unspoken and untold. But without self-awareness, scrutiny and accountability can one honestly say that I am finished, and the examination is done.

Cut! The director screams...a scene well executed and has come to an end. As the main character sits on their chair, left to soak in the reality of life and the salty sweat of deep considerations, become unavoidable.

Released from the restraints of the chair, wrists are bruised along with one's pride and ego. Weakened by the carnival of events and thoughts playing in the mind. I limped off to collect and pick up all the broken pieces.

GENDER WARS

The battle of the sexes between couples and some exes, biting at each other's throats.

Misunderstandings, quarrels and conflicts, contentious name calling and sometimes, "We're doing the MOST!!!!"

How did we get here? The question no one wants to ask, for the truth of the matter is some answers require a task.

And may even reflect our maturity!

Females against males, men rejecting women are the hot topics now on the shows. While marriages decline, leaving families in a bind and divorce is no longer on the back burner.

Individuality is the new hype like getting promotional bars or new stripes, is all that some enjoy and seem to know. We fuss and we fight and are lonely at night but refusing to mature and to grow.

I cherish the old days; our parents had their ways, but never in this state we are in. Like kids who fell out, vexed and with a pout, the silent drop of a pin.

We need to do better my sisters and brothers, for love always starts from within. Ease with the drama let's get together, because in the end...it's good to have a loved one by your side I endorse this and call it a win

TICK TOCK

Ticky Tock the clock stopped, the peeps were in a frenzy, The long wait for the reset became the thing that was trendy.

The hours passed, the times collapsed; the masses awaited a verdict. Of the return to their fun and games like chasing dreams and always pretending.

Minute by minute hour by hour the agony created some tears. Dreams were shot, hopes were crushed and nightmares started new fears.

Finally...!!! hope was on the horizon.

The news was released which created an ease, for the emotional and the uncertain. The curtains were lifted, and the moods were shifted, feeling great to get back on the scene.

Questions were still being asked, like a hero's secret behind the mask, trying to figure out the mysterious task of the TICK, the TOCK and the TOE.

MONEY

Moo-Laa, El dinero, Bread, Stocks, The Bag or Cheese, a universal language everyone understands, acknowledges and agrees.

Empires rise and fall financing desires with ease. Notes accrued by everyone with or without degrees.

Checks, coins, dollars and cents dictate the nominations. We hustle and toil work or grind ,given our own ambitions.

The tech is reigning so supreme the trends follow the flow. While ecommerce has taken the stage with ideas of digital currencies, bitcoins and crypto.

Dolls-Are stacked high on shelves while sense is always in storage. Purchases of expensive goods but can't even afford the mortgage.

Some say it's the root of all evil, but the love of it is in scriptures too. A lot of us have lost our way, chasing the paper, the plastic and jewels.

Just remember money is nice to have but could never, ever, buy a life. Not even love or happiness so be careful when you take a big cut or slice.

TOXIC

Putrid fluids that flow, ooze and leak from septic entities.,
Infected wounds untreated majorities.

Smells of death and decay polluting the air, vilest of rotting
debris more than anyone seems to care.

An unholy mixture of traumatic disorders and broken spirits,
diseases unknown and attitude without cures.

Toxicity runs from sores in the body and leaks out of its pores,
while dirty minds are left to fester as individuals collapse and
melt in their own acidity.

Zombified people with a vicious need to feed, as a new victim
is bitten, it creates a new breed.

Barrels upon barrels of chemical hazards, breaking all the
laws and not adhering to standards. If it continues to spread
and spill; it will contaminate a new generation's mind, body
and soul.

STRANGENESS

There seems to be something that's lurking in the air, it's not normal but rather unsettling and unusually, drear.

The atmosphere feels heavy and weighty with a high sense of gloom, the houses are very empty...and no one occupies their rooms.

Shadows linger in the shade as the sun shines bright as day, while fiending on the unsuspecting prey; to pounce upon and slay.

Souls lost of direction as they wander into darkness, if only there was a glimmer of light to brighten up their starkness.

Dismal minds are laid to waste as imagination takes a flight. While leaving an expensive toll the lights are off each night.

Generation seems disconnected from the things that are humane. While humanity edges towards collapse with focus only on fame.

The good old days and the old school, seemed to be a thing of the past. Overtaken by modern and trendy, these are sure to never last.

I have this feeling of uncertainty as if someone was toying with me, or is this type of strangeness I feel... all just imaginary.

IN YOUR PRESENCE

Last night was magic as we held each other, uncharted hugs, intentionally gripping on my lover. Disconnected from the world around us ,as our eyes met in a romantic laze while everyone and everything was lost in a strongly diluted haze.

I tried to stay focused but was constantly distracted. I'm lost in my thoughts of our own scenes being acted. In your presence the air is soft and sweet, as we share unspoken words our souls connect and meet.

Laughter and love remain constantly here ,as ever so often I steal a subtle stare. I can see your essence speaking to me even though I'm not looking. While guessing what's on that menu of yours, like a five-star chef in the kitchen cooking.

In our presences, yes, I said presences I'm always full of glee. Your smile, your laugh, your gestures are like expensive fragrance sprayed in a Macy's. The whiff makes me' Break-a-neck just to turn around to see.

Being around you I'm always delighted, like a candle-lit dinner on date night that makes the women excited. I pray and hope this experience never comes to an end, because I know I'll be writing poems like these... again and again and again.

PILLOW TALK

After a long hard day settling in for the night, as we reflect on the day's events and rest for dawn's early light. The night is quiet, the moon is still, we share thoughts over the phone with ideas birthed at will.

You lay on your bed, and I lay in mine too, we explore different horizons as destinations start anew. Our pillows are fluffed, and our beds are comfy. We're trying not to laugh so hard to avoid waking anyone and making them grumpy.

The talks are endless, the adventures are set, from topics of the cosmos, life and the first time we met. We talked and talked, wrapped up in conversations for hours, never thinking about time or worrying about tomorrows.

Pillow talk is something unique to the young lovers, couples and maybe a few friends. But one thing is for certain; when a great story starts...it's sure to never come to an end.

WHEN THE RAIN FALLS

When the rain falls, I can feel its songs, its deep drumming and vibrations throughout the test of time. Consistent poundings, Rhythmic expressions, Thoughts revealed memories reflected and clarity refreshed.

When the rain falls, I wonder if the creator expresses its divinity through its showers. When the rain falls, we run with an excitement either to it or from it, while in expressive tones.

When the rainfall words like Wet, Moist, Drizzle, Splash, Plunge, Gloom, Cozy, Comfortable, Windows, Outside, Hard, Heavy and Storm are used frequently.

And finally, when the rain falls, I'm constantly reminded of how great the things in the universe are, and how we are all; somehow interconnected and interdependent on each other. From the rains which fall on the inside to the rains that fall on the outside the waters are always a part of us.

A DELICIOUS CUP of JO' ANNE

As the sun kisses the early dawn my eyes are opened as I turn and yawn. What is this delightful desire that stirs in my tummy? Is it for the dark deliciousness on my tongue makes me say yummy?

She's tall, dark and delicious just the way I like it brewed, with the sweetest of aromas that makes you feel renewed. OH, some love dark liquor before they eat and shower, but if it was up to me, I drink her every hour.

Others prefer it a little sweet, maybe with hints of milk, but when it comes down to my cup of JO, She's satisfyingly smooth as silk hmmmmm! The sweetness of her dark essence is rich and full, especially when it's Brazilian not decaffeinated or espresso.

I'd never stopped drinking my dark delicious indulgent brew, because it has me feeling so full filled and leaving so renewed. From the very first sip, until the very last drop. I'll always need that hot cup of JO...that wakes me and keeps me on top.

MY SOULMATE

Morning coffee is sweet and enriching, as I crave my soul mate's delicious milk. Two scoops, oh wait! No sugar needed as we will burn through all those calories.

I am teared open, like a fresh pack of Brazilian, to be pounded, grounded and ready to serve hot. My lips gently kiss the dark nectar of your cup, whistling off the steamy indulgences.

One cup, two cups, three cups, four my soulmate returns home craving for more. Never drinking the "teas" oh please! let me have my coffee with ice, as it cools me right on down and makes me feel so nice.

My soulmate and I stay tied and connected, like a moth to a flame we're always directed. By the burning passion and unavoidable allure, the love we make will always remain pure.

My soulmate's kitchen I shall always return; I love playing with the fire but never get burned. I love coming to dine again and again, because of that hot cup of coffee; along with that good home cooking... Man! it makes me come back with my plate always looking.

SWEET FINGERPRINTS

Clickety click on the keyboard of life, Mother Nature, she types these scripts of destinies to unfold. She gazes at her own works repeatedly and makes new, or improved adjustments.

She arranges each plan to be in synchronicity, arranging the blueprints of life in sweet symmetry and harmonious symphony. She toils with the rhythm of the ancient echoes in the light of the universe.

Her version is unique, and her vision is directed by the cosmos. As she 'ENTERS' the plans of life within the world. 'BACKSPACE' the errors of corruption, chaos and confusion. 'UPSHIFT' Greatness into being and 'DOWNSHIFT' for real reflections. 'DOUBLE CLICKING' To create new opportunities.

She pressed 'DELETE' On the things in her plan-et which offered no purpose or value to her grand design. Then she relaxes on her throne admiring the work of our hands.

THE SPILL

News spreads like wildfire rushing to capture her soul, malicious words of warning from deceptive paparazzi. Their thirst for 'the spill' possesses no regard and has no limit.

Just wanting to be left alone, just for a few, but can't seem to get a minute or two. They Stampede her through the lens and flashes; hoping to get a new scoop but not from her face, eyes and lashes.

Hounds! roaming around the grounds, within her perimeters. Sharking for new bites in the ocean of risk and opportunity. Watching and waiting patiently for a new meal to surface.

Getting 'The spill' is all that matters to them; as the attainment of it, taints credibility and destroys characters. She often moves in the shadows because she doesn't want to be overshadowed.

Her eyes seem weary, as you look right in it. The frustration shows underneath her smiles and under the spotlight for her, is never evasive. Because in the end they never cared about her feelings, all they need is... 'The spill' to tarnish your dreams.

GRATITUDE FOR EXISTENCE

Hey universe, how are you today? we never ask how you're doing, and only care about the things we do and the promises we make.

Hey universe, can I talk to you for a minute? Can I tell you thank you for everything that you have done and how far you've brought me through. Can I thank you for holding my hand and creating my existence; as part of your master plan?

Hey, I know sometimes, I forget that you are in control, when things don't go as planned. I get flustered and full of regret but somehow you know how to always keep me on track; and before you know it I always bounce right back.

Hey universe, thank you for never giving up on me when others saw a failure. You taught me what I could be. When the mountain top seemed high and the valleys felt low. You give me wisdom, knowledge and understanding so that I could learn, heal and even grow.

Hey universe, forgive me if I'm ungrateful and forget to thank you for the life that I have; because I am normal and physically able. It's unfortunate some are born with disabilities, I need to appreciate life's simplicities.

Hey universe, thank you for having this talk with me ,because sometimes I really need your help, support and therapy. Help *this poem to touch the lives that it will, reflecting on appreciation for all good things still.*

IF I SHOULD DIE BEFORE I WRITE

If I should die before I write, remember the pen in my hand that drew the dreams of insight.

Remember the poetic art we created together and how the pen constantly mated with the paper.

Remember when I wrote and sometimes lost my focus, but still continue to write different stories that's ...supposed to!

Remember the hearts, minds and souls that were touched, especially when I wrote the ideas that made me laugh so much.

Remember the grand times we had writing, to uplift and inspire those who felt sad. Because lives were touched, making them feel happy, wonderful and glad.

Finally Remember me not as a versatile poet, but just someone who wanted you to love life ;and be an inspiration to show it.

Remember Me... if I should die before I write not just me but the legacy.

I JUST WANT TO BE ME

I just want to be me, not defined by any labels. I just want to be me and not sit at your fancy tables.

Respect me for who I am and not what you want me to be, because your vision is skewed and tinted; which does not reflect my identity.

I just want to be free from your ideas, perception and presumptions. Just seen for the person I am, with honesty and pure intentions never reflecting fakeness or shams.

I just want to be me, and no I'm not asking for too much, a lot of us tried to be someone else and become soulfully out of touch.

I will definitely continue to be me, not defined by your words or any of your labels, because a lot of times no one wants to listen; to all your stories and resonate with your fables.

I will peel them off and shake them loose because I will never be tied up in chaos or hung by your noose.

ADDICTION

My mind is in a constant flux. I'm truly in an endless daze; constantly lost for words as my days perish.

Sitting staring into nothingness, as the thoughts of you creep into my psyche, forever consumed by your existence.

Feigning seems like child's play since hit after hit is never enough. The price paid is never too much or never too high...just because it's the good stuff.

You are my personal pharmacist, always knowing just what to prescribe, without knowing you know, and without showing you show a true professional at work.

Addiction doesn't even feel like the right word, since I can feel you in my veins as my body calls out for more. I pop you like I pop pills fresh out of the card.

Sometimes I wonder if I will ever be cured, get tired or fed up with my habit. Then I realized that I was addicted from the moment I laid eyes on you.

GREEDY FOR MY MAN

Yes, I said it. I know I'm greedy for him not because of his bank account or the thing in his pants.

It's the time he takes to be attentive to me, and listens to my issues in a world that's full of demands

Yes, I said it, I'm the greedy one you better stop staring, before I sucker punch you in the throat, when your eyes are glaring.

He's sweet and possesses a unique type of charm. I love when he hugs me and his hands keep me warm.

I love cooking for him and catering to whatever he wants. He never looks at you heifers With the BBL you flaunt.

I love my man, he's my kind of guy, never worry about him leaving because he comes right home with hugs and kisses. To cut his sweet chocolate pie.

So, call me greedy, even a bit needy but when it comes to my baby, I love supporting him gladly. He's my rock, my fortress, the shoulder that I lean on. When I'm lost, he leads me with his vision.

So, if you want to know why I glow, because you're slow, the love we have for each other will always grow. He lets me be greedy for him again and again because he knows I'm gonna be better than these other women.

DEW'S PEACEFUL REST

Her dreams are of the universe; untouched and untainted by human hands. Mother Nature continually nurtures her daughter... 'DEW' as her name is called.

She was created in the wee hours of the morning and taken away before the day's crack of dawn, to be cradled elsewhere from unseen eyes.

Her playmates are the flowers, plants, trees and tall grass all who are touched by her hands; as they gather to play in the stillness of the night reflecting the previous day.

If you're lucky to be an early bird, sometimes you may find her at rest, just before the sun comes out and you start becoming your best.

She disappeared throughout the day; where neither even her parents or peers could find her. They sometimes weep from scattered clouds...with thoughts as if they timed her.

Alas she tiptoed in the night catching them all fast asleep, greeting them with gentle hugs and kisses ,waking them up to meet.

IN THE CORNER

As I sit in the corner reflecting and staring at you the camera flashes on my essence. The lines blur as the background tells endless stories about many encounters.

Looking through the lens back at me I can feel your eyes piercing at the possibilities while unique poses, responded effortlessly.

The contrast is stunning; the connections between reflections offer creativity wrapped up in film.

My beautiful eyes, full lips and natural hair presents a welcomed aesthetics, as my smooth soft skin enhances the quality of your vision. With each flashing, harmony is met with the solidification memories.

I shall forever be remembered through the ages. As the one who sat in the corner creating...the world around her.

YOUR POTENTIAL

Divine purpose woven into your very fabric, the puzzle is complete; and the picture is clear. Achievement sets the stage and the pathways become clearer as desire burns a bright flame.

Unshaken by the distractions and darkness the vision provokes drive, uniquely positioned to attain results unfathomable.

Your potential is part of "SELF" created by selfishness, but tremendously far from it. Fulfilling the scripts of the universe and bringing reasons into life.

Rewritten decisions that were once crafted in stone, seldomly exist as ambitions are realized.

Never allowing a premature death of dreams, as the fight of survival establishes destiny. In the final chapter "YOUR POTENTIAL is YOU and YOU are your POTENTIAL."

THE HEART

The heart is in constant need of repair, from the fractures of its broken foundations...creating emotional despair.

Valves become blocked with hatred, dishonesty and pride. While the blood thinners that are taken, offer forgiveness to flow inside.

Cardiology is the class taken to help cope and deal with the strain; because people think it's "the matters of the heart" when truly, it's the thoughts of the brain.

Chambers carry vital stuff reminiscent of things from the past, while skipping beats of rhythmic thumps without subtle lust and mask.

A heart attack is never seen but its pain is felt inside. The enlarged heart with swollen veins tell unspoken truths; where the underlying secrets hide.

I shall fix, restore and protect this heart of mine; because it's the only one that I am given. And try my best to do what's right...since it reflects how I am living.

DESERVE

Deserve?... A term that's frequently well overused, I know it because it's probably tired. From the audience's audacity of saying "I definitely deserve this, and I definitely deserve that", but no one seems to be buying.

When did we become so obsessed with entitlement, as if inheritance alone was a win; because things like character, personality, kindness and being yourself are regarded more as our twin.

If anything! in life you truly 'deserve'; is to be the best authentic version of (YOU) this you can always be. In the end our time is limited and short, cause we take too long to figure out and see.

You deserve to be alive here and now, to learn, change and to grow. So, forget about the meaningless and material things. Their seeds are lifeless distractions where no wisdom can never be...bestowed.

GREATNESS

What makes us great as we sit and reflect; is it the cars, clothes and houses we buy our erect?

Is it the way we carry ourselves or the way that we walk, some might even say it's our confident smiles, along with the way that we talk.

Does your 'GREATNESS' show only when you get a win, or is it expected even when your patience is running thin?

The 'GREATNESS' you have does it make you feel better, or do you crave more through the admiration of others?

'GREATNESS' should be sourced, from only deep down inside. Where the best things are made and forged, cultivating a sense of pride.

'GREATNESS' can never be bought or sold, it's neither new nor old, but every time you look into the mirror; just remember when you say your prayers,…'GREATNESS' is staring straight back at you.

YOU DO ME... WITHOUT DOING ME!

You do me without doing me, these are the thoughts that play in my head. It's like you've got me in a chokehold. I definitely crave your prescribed MEDS.

I went to get a full checkup to figure out what's happening to my brain. The doctors said they can't find anything wrong with me, and the thoughts of you came rushing again.

I tried talking to a psychiatrist because I thought I needed a little therapy, then I spoke with the preacher about it, but he responded I'll see you on Sunday!...I decided to speak to my DAD about it and he said, "Boy you ain't got no clue, cause those symptoms that you are experiencing happens to all men too."

He laughed and said you'll be fine; your heart is in the right place but as he spoke, I saw thoughts of you dancing and laughing with a beautiful smile on your face.

You've done something to me I know! but in a good kind of way. I'm still trying to figure it out cause maybe it's your kindness and love which fills my darkest of days and takes away my pout.

Or maybe! Perhaps it's your genuine, gentle personality that sets the tone in a room. It could even be the fragrances that you wear which hint at designer perfumes.

Whatever it is, I really don't care, because I'm trying not to lose any sleep. Cause you do me without doing me, and we weren't wrapped up in the sheets.

THE LIGHT

Peek-a-boo!... "Welcome my little one" As a mother receives her imprint into the tainted consciousness of our world.

The big bright lights of arrival are met by showers of emotions, judgments and scrutiny. As onlookers await the visuals and the resounding songs of innocence.

A quick smack on the bottom, awakened by reality to initiate the respiratory responses. The ignition of life begins with dynamic breathes, releasing soft cries; distinct but yet familiar to those of old.

Moms discerning eye looks with deep emotional intention, care and warmth. They are void of pain and free of exhaustion from labors toiled. Unconditional, the connection made before conception.

Uncertainties, worries and prayers pave the pathways between one's entrance into this world and before our exit out of life. For her love has never left us...orphaned.

Cleaned, wrapped and surrendered into familiar arms as excited audible messages are transmitted. The sounds of love through one's tiny little ears, toes curling; as eyes blink and stare searching for innate recognitions.

FATHER, waits patiently to enter the room on cue, overwhelmingly elated. The universe appoints his legacies, giving names of meaning tradition and ancestry. While he stares into the eyes of the next generations.

Parenthood begins; the 1st chapter is written, now they both will have to navigate the seas together. Learning as they go; and growing with maturity for there is no manual for a life...DIRECTLY!

THE NEW CHAPTER

Turning the pages destiny awaits, like ships setting up to sail the captain signals the mates.

The sails are raised and the adventure is new; a seasoned captain shall charter destinations within view.

A new chapter begins on an epic voyage; the rations are grand and stacked within the storage.

Challenges are bound as obstacles are presented, navigating the seas with skill precision intended.

Sleepless nights and endless days, lost at times in many different kinds of ways. The travel is rough and the waves are heavy; as we keep her afloat and stare her steady.

Alas! the shore is seen as the vision becomes clear, the anchor is lowered for the land is near.

Disembarking on the island; the captain and his crew. What treasures might lie ahead to gather; infinitely many...and never a few.

GRAND RISING - "EVERYDAY"

Everyday is an opportunity to be better, so stop worrying about what others have to say or even the weather.

Everyday is a chance we all have been given, so let's embrace it and just start living.

Everyday the sun shines in its glory, and it's time for us to write and create our own stories.

Every morning there's always another day of hope, so just don't lie in bed with a frown and mope.

Everyday nothing is promised to you and me, but the possibilities are endless if we are willing to try and seek.

Everyday I will be grateful and thankful forever in the smallest of ways.

Because in the end, I never know when my time will be up as the creator, numbers my days.

THE WARMTH

The warmth of your love kisses my thoughts intentionally each and every day.

My smiles keep on bursting with Glee, leaving me speechless looking for what to say.

I'm constantly excited when I'm thinking of you. The little things you say and the wonderful things you do.

You never bore me, even though you are asking. Just keep being you sexy, spontaneous and creatively everlasting.

Each day I'm grateful for the time we spend on hand, trusting the creator to fulfill our desires and master our plans.

You are my soul mate and this you'll forever be, because the warmth of your love changes me for the better... ever so increasingly.

EARLY MORNING PLEASURES

What is this sweetness that cracks across my face, and makes me smile without a waste; Is it a sweet scent or warm embrace?

She greets me softly and gently as the break of dawn, with the sweetest of spirits that cascade.

I am constantly in awe, like dew kissed flowers welcoming a new era.

Morning pleasures are indeed her essence and her positive attitude gives a flavorful presence.

I love her mornings because she is the best, the awakening of a goddess separated from the rest.

HEY YOU!

When I was young, I was told to use my imagination never was I taught that this was the essence of my creation.

As a young boy I dreamt of many toys and while I was growing, they were my favorite joys.

As a young lad never thinking my dreams would come true, I thought of Mansions, fast Cars, Skyscrapers to own and even Helicopters just to name a few.

Now well into my Adolescence dreams become different, hormonal imbalances, girls and times well spent. Biology at work but doesn't pay rent.

Finally, I'm a man now and many of my dreams have come true? Yes, to be exact just to give a clue. I got the girl, the family and the life I always wanted and yes if you can believe from a simple dream the seeds were planted.

BODY CANVAS

Let me paint a perfect picture in the viewing of your mind. Her body is so shapely a masterpiece, one-of-a-kind.

I apply my brush to put the lines in the right places; with contours here, blending there and fades in precise spaces. We start with a face as bright as the moon and hair flowing like the wind. Then the eyes, big, bright and beautiful, carry a glow from within.

A smile of the ages that cracked the coldest of hearts, while the neck and shoulders connect in sync, like a supporting actor playing their part.

Full supple breast like chocolate kissed mountains, put a (suckle) grin on your face that would make you drink from her fountain.

A tummy that's smooth and soft without uneven lines, just like the plains of an African Savannah without trees or low hanging vines.

Hips that cascade the waist of creation, by way which we've come, generations after generations birthed into the sun.

Legs thick and terrific that carry a vessel of power, giving support like tall trees, strong like divine towers.

Not forgetting her perched Cliffs at the back, we stare at them from miles away, as you come closer to the scenery within view...the vision is here to stay.

Picasso completed - body canvas!

HANDS OF THE UNIVERSE

What is this dark matter and what is it that makes the moon and stars stay in endlessness...infinitely?

Is this the work of the hands of the universe; where planets are formed, stars collapse, expansion and implosions?

Unknown ideas being birthed and destiny established into existence. What majesty is this?

Oh Hands of the universe, thou hast created the wonders of the skys, the seen and unseen, the known and unknown, the finite and infinite.

Wonders continued to stretch the imagination, beyond the boundlessness of possibilities; mixed in with tangible probabilities.

Hands of the universe we adore the distant twinkles and the bright sparkles of the things which give rise... to be named.

OH! dear hands of the universe, you continue to leave us speechless and deeply wowed with divine splendor. Gratitude, thankfulness and appreciation for your glorious displays. Humbling every moment within time.

From eternity to eternity, from the east to the West, from the north to the South, from creation to creation, from Galaxy to galaxies, and from universe to multiverses. We owe you your atoms and everything, even our end... respect, OH hands of the universe.

WILD SUMMER NIGHTS

The heat has risen and the night is alive. People seem to be everywhere as the nightclubs seem to thrive.

Naked bodies out and about trying to cool off from the heat. Bumping and grinding at parties to the vibes of every beat. Sweat running down as we dance and we twirl, while the onlookers say, "damn look at all those girls!"

Whether it's a night at the beach as the waves roll in slowly, touching our footsteps to reach. Or whether at a campfire in the mountains, where we sing at night and by the day drink at fountains.

Maybe it's even a cool nice drive to the city at night, to bar hop with friends and get drinks and maybe start or part a few fights. Why does the summer nights take so long to get here with the 'heat on tilt' and it's too hot for blankets or a quilt?

Sometimes we sit on the porch, the steps outside and even on the sidewalk, listening to some music and greeting the passers-by and the little dogs that bark. At night the ice cream truck may roam the streets for the ladies and kids to grab their treats.

A cone here and a popsicle there, will have everyone giving a few subtle stares. All these wild summer nights when the moon is just right, lively essence in plain sight. Some vacation and still, and some at home, some partying in the backyard and some on their phones.

I will continue to love these wild summer nights, because they always create memories as each summer continues to come. Throughout the centuries we are creating more memories. So just remember when the place is hot and the mood is just right, hold the one you love and enjoy these wild summer nights.

TIME

If time is so precious, then why do we waste it. We wasted by either doing nothing or worrying about stupid ****. We waste it with senseless arguments and silent phone calls.

Hateful conversations with imaginary walls. We waste it so much knowing we can get it back. With all this knowledge we have, why does it seem like we lack it?

We need to make better use of our time as we never know when it will be up. We need to fill it with memories and let it overflow our cup.

Time waits on no one, that's why it's always running. Let's use it more wisely instead of thoughts that are so cunning.

Life is short, memories are great. Fill them with love and joy and reduce the amount of hate.

Make the memories you have shine in your heart, so that you'll remember that 'TIME' and feel the love and happiness from the start.

Our time is here, and our time is now, no sense asking questions of who, what, when and how. Enjoy the moments with the ones you love before they're just a memory with prayer hands and a dove.

Live in the moment and enjoy each and every day. Start being appreciative. It's a grateful heart while your time is here to stay. So don't get upset too frequently and waste your time. Just take a breather and relax, and who knows you may remember this rhyme.

REFLECTIVE THOUGHTS

1. THE TRAIN RIDE

2.

Today I was on the train... I usually don't find being on my phone entertaining. However, interestingly I was on the train making my usual observations within a discrete manner of course, and whilst doing this out of nowhere a thought came to me. I glanced around and in a split second; remembered the media and topics about racism. What am I really getting at or what is it that I am really saying?

Well Simply put; we argue, criticize, condemn and constantly be at each other's throats, and here I am on a train every day, with everyone embodying the reality That we are all simply just humans. Everyday a mixture of diverse cultures, sit side by side, asking questions, giving directions, Saying, "excuse me please!", Giving up seats to the elderly, strangers, expectant mothers and cracking jokes etcetera.

And yet out of all this social Communion we disembark to go our various ways and "delete each other" in cold blood and sometimes without remorse. The reality of my thoughts Allowed me to take a more in depth look at the unexplainable, unpredictable and sheer complexity of human behavior. We Are truly something else; we delete the people who help us...

Food for thought not to cause any offense but for reflection purposes only.

THANK YOU.

REFLECTIVE THOUGHTS Cont'd

3. IT'S BEEN A WHILE

4.

It's been a while as usual but today I awoke feeling humble and grateful. Why might you ask? Well to answer your question I get the chance every day to be part of this wonderful existence or what some may refer to as the terrestrial plane. I reflect conscientiously on the things right in front of me, the sunlight, the air that we breathe, the plants and animals and the rain when it falls. It's amazing how everything works In Sync when it comes to nature.

I usually find myself pondering and you're probably wondering what I am getting at? Well, it's simple Out of all the planets in the solar system, Milky Way, Galaxies, The cosmos etcetera. Science teaches us that so far only our planet 'EARTH' possesses the uniqueness of having all the requirements which work in a synchronized way of sustaining, creating and replicating life perfectly! Whether this statement is true or not this isn't consequential for the purpose of my deliberations.

Now let's just stop for a moment, I came across a documentary one time that stated there was a certain satellite which identified about 13 planets that may possess or possibly possess the potential for life... but these planets in short, were nothing like ours. I am not looking for an audience or anyone to subscribe to my thoughts. My innate Cosmetic makeup allows me to understand that there is a reason for everything. Some refer to that reason as God, science or some greater influence, or whatever "it" is. I say thank you for allowing me the opportunity of being a part of this master PLAN kind of In Sync with the word PLAN-ET just saying.

And finally remember to be your best, do your best, and forget about the rest. This was your Author, Poet and Friend.

LOVE OF MY...LOVE

What is this that I feel, Is this Love of my love, truly something real. Is it this kind of thing that keeps my heart pounding?

It stood the test of time, creating eternal memories, the love of my love lasts longer than centuries.

The love of my love will forever grow stronger, as we shall navigate through mazes. The exploration of new journeys chartered, together, completing life's phases.

The love of my love, our love shall always remain complete. Deliciously presented like one of my favorite dishes or treats.

Love of my love, you are my heart in this life and the next, I hope you will continue to prosper in love...void of evil or hex.

BONUS ITEM

PATRIOTIC

A word that makes us feel a sense of Obligation;whether to our own demons or to a nation.

The very thing that sets us apart from every other, can make onlookers scoff and mock...and not even care to bother.

Are we true believers of the pledges,decrees,promises and oaths that we make ? Or maybe when it's time to stand on their values, we bow our heads in shame for bribes and grants we take.

Building a strong nation starts from within the home; or did we forget this! seeking our independent ways alone. We are always a reflection for the world to see, whether looking into the mirror, social media and on T.V.

Patriotism is the study that explains who,when,where, why and what we are. Regardless of whether we live in countries near or afar.

INJUSTICE

UNFAIRNESS -Beyond the highest degree leaves the brain in turmoil and the mind wondering.

INEQUITY - transparent with dark deliberations from those ,that whole ultimate power.

CORRUPTION - Beyond variant degrees from individuals to communities, its infection rate spreads faster than any disease.

CRUELTY - is established beyond measure and seen throughout the world, as gems are taken to the slaughter house by swines who trampled on pearls.

BRUTALITY - is evident and everywhere as the cuts and bruises revealed the truth;While beatings, abuse and violence are products of every brute.

TYRANNY - overtakes populous since fairness, morale and honor becomes invisible. This leaves people unable to contain themselves leaving the door..."irresponsible"

DESPOTISM - sits on a pinnacle and overlooks the masses, while delegating instruction of Chaos imposing; devilish maskings.

REPRESSION - becomes a coping mechanism for their atrocities, That have been committed. The feelings of aggression, vexation and toleration constantly put a strain on the seal.

SUPPRESSION - can only last for so long before the pipe bursts or the whistle blows. Sometimes even evidence is hidden in plain sight, preventing the truth we know.

EXPLOITATION - is a regular practice for those controlling the products or services. They make you pay a heavy price just to give you a thin cut or quarter of a slice.

BIAS - is seen and ascertained within the reportsBy the certain and the uncertain. " Wild stories" are told with unfavorable tones and deeply mixed emotions.

PREJUDICE - breeds prejudgments based on limited views and presumptions. These continue to instill fear with ignorance about their perceptions.

BIGOTRY - is rooted in racism instead of humanity and nature, creating demonic influence and feeding the Young without compassion, empathy and structure.

FAVORITISM - belongs to a selective few as you can never be a part of The Clique or the group. Special gifts are consistently presented to dedicated members of the crew.

PARTIALITY - runs rampant within regimes especially when you're not part of the class. Like tinted windows, true intentions are hidden behind the glass.

PARTISANSHIP - establishes the mission for complete adherence to, and compromise in favor of the 'PEOPLE' suffering beyond reproach.

INTOLERANCE - speaks of the inability to tolerate the slackness, dishonesty and disrespect. festering mood swings of many sorts fueled by hate and regret.

WRONG - is seen as a different thing these days, maybe even a thing of the past; and "RIGHT"Sometimes becomes questionable when tinted in mysteries to grasp.

INJURY - reaches, the mind, body, and so not just the physical too! the far-reaching repercussions imprinted, can last this generation or even a few.

OFFENSE - is often caused by a breach of law and also even the feeling the provocations that increase between the two, will create disastrous dealings.

EVIL - does not only refer to spirits, but immorality and wickedness too. Many are corruptly indoctrinated, selling their souls at the pews.Forgetting the high price paid for riches; trickle the dollars a few.

VILLAINY - is Criminal Behavior conducted by those that are high ranking. It started when those who are in authority, require a serious spanking.

CRIME - is like a fire that is started, ignited by a little Spark. who forgot it can happen in daylight; because some believe it only lives in the dark.

SIN - is a transgression against Divine Law, a deliberate Act of disobedience and a failure to do what's right. The blood of the innocent intentionally spilled, will definitely bring us a plight.

INIQUITY - seems to be rampant, since the conscience of the powerful are seared; leaving them open and vulnerable for the vengeance about to be prepared.

MISDEED - Something many will run from and end up at their own demise. anything that is done in the dark will be seen by the brightest star/ Spark.

OUTRAGE - is the cry of the broken hearted, whose voices have not been heard. They gather together with their armies, their Legions in numbers unheard.

ATROCITY - highly unpleasant and distasteful is the way life is cherished these days; We massacre, destroy and pillage the foundations our ancestors, carefully paved always.

SCANDAL - whispered The Echoes of the unspoken voices lost in the shadows. their truths resonate throughout the grapevines of humanity.

DISGRACE - is an understatement only to describe the feelings of those who are senior to the actions of what is transpiring. Leaving a sour taste and bitter endings on the town.

MONSTROSITY - is the best way to describe the behavior of those who were placed with the power to lead by example, but instead they play the victim to their sinful desires and dark motivations.

AFFRONT - is an action or remark that causes an outrage or offense. This can never be remedied by putting on a plaster over a gaping womb.

(GRIEVANCE - is a feeling of resentment over something believed to be wrong or unfair; a real or imagined wrong or other cause for complaint, or protests, especially unfair treatment. Definitions by Google)

"Be your best , Do your best ! and Forget about the rest."

www.ingramcontent.com/pod-product-compliance
Lightning Source LLC
Chambersburg PA
CBHW050414030726
47503CB00006B/2186